FELIPE and CLAUDETTE

FELIPE and CLAUDETTE

BY MARK TEAGUE

SCHOLASTIC INC.

On adoption day, all the pets at the animal shelter lined up for inspection.

"It is time," said Mrs. Barrett, the director, "for us to look our best!"

Then one by one they were adopted, until only two pets remained: Felipe and Claudette.

"What will I do with you?" fretted Mrs. Barrett. Usually, her pets were adopted quickly, but not these two. They had been at the shelter for ages.

The problem, in Felipe's opinion, was Claudette. "You will never be adopted," he told the dog, "because you are constantly barking."

"What?" Claudette barked. "What what what?"

To be fair, Claudette did not always bark.
Sometimes she tore the stuffing from her toys.

Sometimes she ran in circles.

Sometimes she bounced against the walls.

She drove Felipe crazy. "Please," he said, "I am trying to think."
He was trying to think about his future home. Perhaps it would
be a beautiful country estate, where he might lounge beside a
pool . . . or maybe a penthouse apartment, where he would eat
sardines from a dainty bowl.

Claudette belched and the dream faded. "No," said Felipe, when she brought him her ball. "I will not throw your little ball. It is covered in spittle. Anyway, cats do not throw."

More puppies came
to the shelter, then more
kittens. Soon it was
adoption day again.

"Time to look our best!" cried Mrs. Barrett. They did and
they were all adopted.
All except Felipe and Claudette.
"What will I do with you two?" worried Mrs. Barrett.

Felipe thought she should worry about Claudette. "You will never be adopted," he told the dog, "because you snore when you are wide-awake."

"Snork?" snored Claudette. "Snork snork snork?"

To be fair, Claudette did not always snore.

Sometimes she dug holes in the yard.

Sometimes she chased moths.

Sometimes she rolled in the garbage.

She drove Felipe mad. It would be difficult for either of them to be adopted when Claudette made such a poor impression. She brought him a toy.

"No, I will not play tug-of-war," said Felipe. "Cats do not tug."

More kittens came to the shelter, then more puppies. Adoption day arrived again. Felipe groomed his fur and straightened his whiskers.

Claudette wagged her tail. One by one, the pets were adopted.

All except Felipe and Claudette.

"Dear, dear," said Mrs. Barrett. "What will I do with you two?"

It was clear to Felipe that Claudette was the problem. "You will never be adopted," he said, "as long as you have dried dog food stuck to your nose."

"Slurp?" said Claudette, licking her nose. "Slurp slurp slurp?"

To be fair, Claudette did not always have dried dog food stuck to her nose.

Sometimes she had branches stuck to her collar.

Sometimes she had leaves stuck to her paws.

Sometimes her whole body was covered with mud.

She drove Felipe insane. What could he do with a dog like her? She wagged her tail hopefully.

"No, I will not play hide-and-seek," said Felipe. "I do not wish to be 'it.' Anyway, it is perfectly obvious where you are hiding."

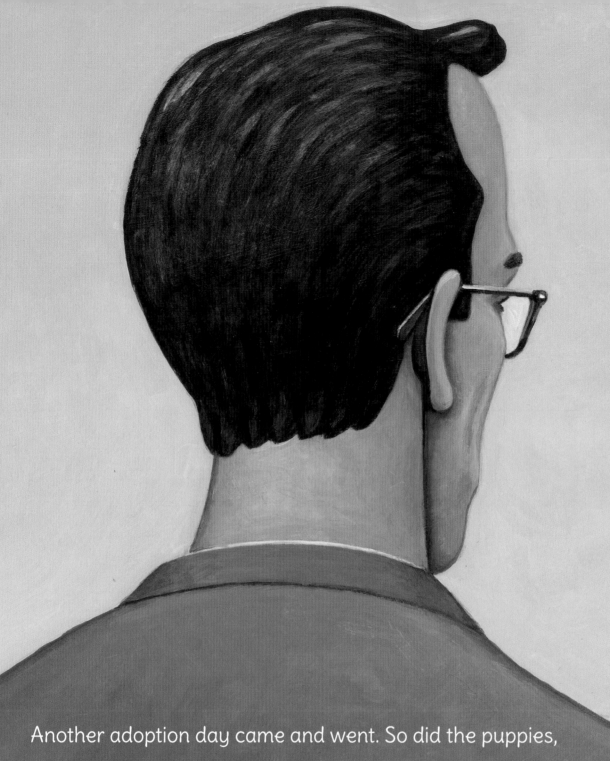

Another adoption day came and went. So did the puppies, so did the kittens. As usual, only Felipe and Claudette remained. Mrs. Barrett was closing the shelter when a gentleman arrived.

"I wish to adopt a pet," he said. Felipe sat up straight.

"We only have the two," said Mrs. Barrett. "Felipe is quiet, but a bit grumpy."

"And the dog?' asked the man.

"Claudette barks and chews and digs holes in the yard."

"Anything else?"

"She runs in circles and rolls in garbage and snores
when she is wide-awake."
"Fine," said the gentleman. "I'll take her."
And he did.

Felipe was stunned. Who in their right mind would adopt Claudette?

"You miss her, don't you?" said Mrs. Barrett.

Certainly not, thought Felipe. He waited for the next adoption day.

And he waited.

And he waited.

Time passed slowly. The animal shelter seemed very quiet.
He stared at Claudette's toys and her ball and her empty bowl.
"I'm sure she's fine," said Mrs. Barrett.
Felipe sighed.

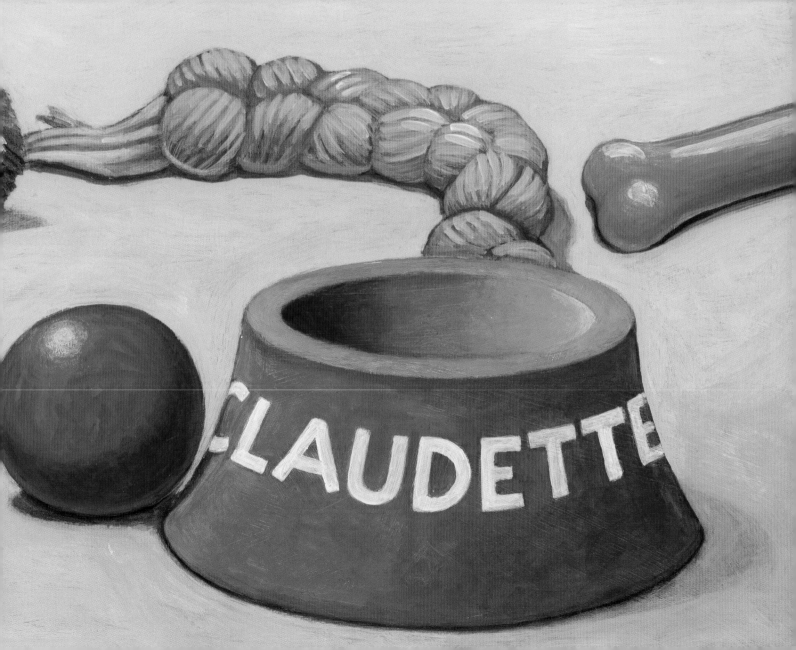

Adoption day came. The puppies went. So did the kittens. Felipe hid in the back room. After a while, Mrs. Barrett joined him. She was closing the shelter when the gentleman returned with Claudette. "I am bringing her back," he said. "She is not the dog I thought she was. She doesn't play or chew or run in circles. She doesn't even bark. All she does is mope."

As soon as he left, Claudette began to bark. She licked Mrs. Barrett. She chased Felipe around the room.

"What will I do with you two?" said Mrs. Barrett, but really, it was obvious. She adopted them. For dinner, she fed them sardines in dainty bowls. Afterward they played hide-and-seek.

Felipe was happy to be "it."